P9-DGG-361

BKM
Guelph Public Library
JP BAR
Barnett, Mac.
The Great Zapfino
April 01, 2022
33281021250557

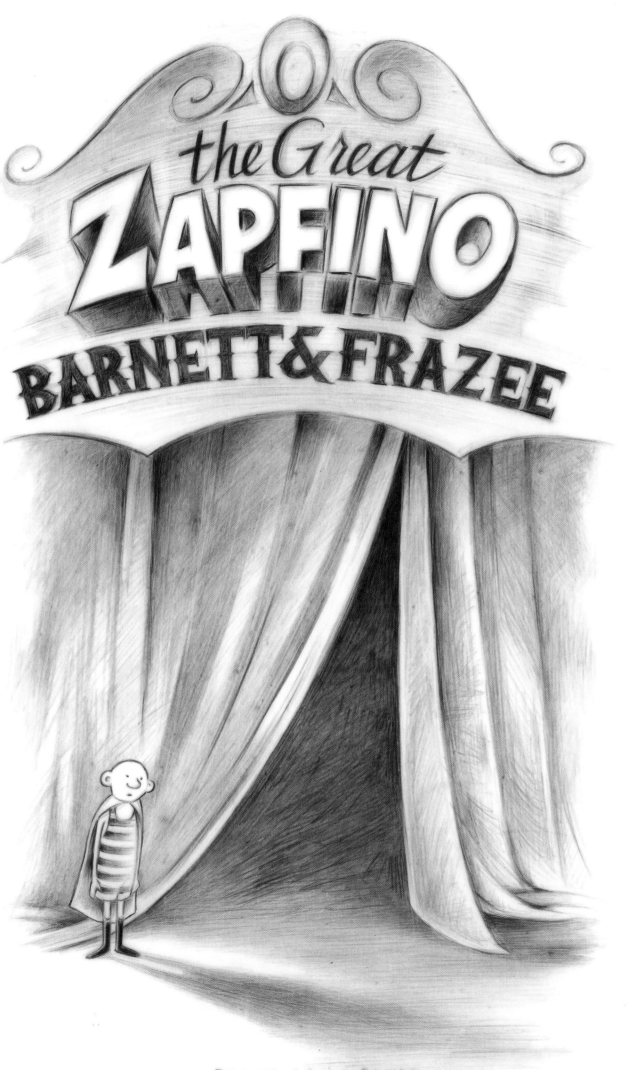

the Great ZAPFINO

BARNETT & FRAZEE

BEACH LANE BOOKS
NEW YORK   LONDON   TORONTO   SYDNEY   NEW DELHI

JP
BAR

For Mom — M.B.
For my weirdo — M.F.

BEACH LANE BOOKS
An imprint of Simon & Schuster Children's Publishing Division
1230 Avenue of the Americas, New York, New York 10020
Text © 2022 by Mac Barnett
Illustration © 2022 by Marla Frazee
Book design by Marla Frazee and Lauren Rille © 2022 by Simon & Schuster, Inc.
All rights reserved, including the right of reproduction in whole or in part in any form.
BEACH LANE BOOKS and colophon are trademarks of Simon & Schuster, Inc.
For information about special discounts for bulk purchases,
please contact Simon & Schuster Special Sales at 1-866-506-1949
or business@simonandschuster.com.
The Simon & Schuster Speakers Bureau can bring authors to your live event.
For more information or to book an event, contact the
Simon & Schuster Speakers Bureau at 1-866-248-3049
or visit our website at www.simonspeakers.com.
The text for this book was hand lettered by Marla Frazee.
The illustrations for this book were rendered in black Prismacolor pencil on Dura-Lar matte film.
Manufactured in China
0122 SCP
First Edition
10 9 8 7 6 5 4 3 2 1
Library of Congress Cataloging-in-Publication Data
Names: Barnett, Mac, author. | Frazee, Marla, illustrator.
Title: The Great Zapfino / Mac Barnett ; illustrated by Marla Frazee.
Description: First edition. | New York : Beach Lane Books, [2022] | Audience: Ages 0-8. | Audience:
Grades 2-3. | Summary: To escape a burning building, Zapfino must confront the fears that forced
him out of the circus.
Identifiers: LCCN 2021003797 (print) | LCCN 2021003798 (ebook) | ISBN 9781534411548
(hardcover) | ISBN 9781534411555 (ebook)
Subjects: CYAC: Fear—Fiction. | Circus—Fiction. | Fire—Fiction.
Classification: LCC PZ7.B26615 Gr 2022 (print) | LCC PZ7.B26615 (ebook) | DDC [E]—dc23
LC record available at https://lccn.loc.gov/2021003797
LC ebook record available at https://lccn.loc.gov/2021003798

And now, before your very eyes, the Great Zapfino will perform the thrilling LEAP FOR LIFE.

Prepare to gasp as Zapfino dives ten terrifying stories through the air, landing on a tiny t r a m p o l i n e !

Zapfino will dodge peril and brave calamity in an impossible feat of derring-do! Watch in awe as Zapfino defies fate for your entertainment.

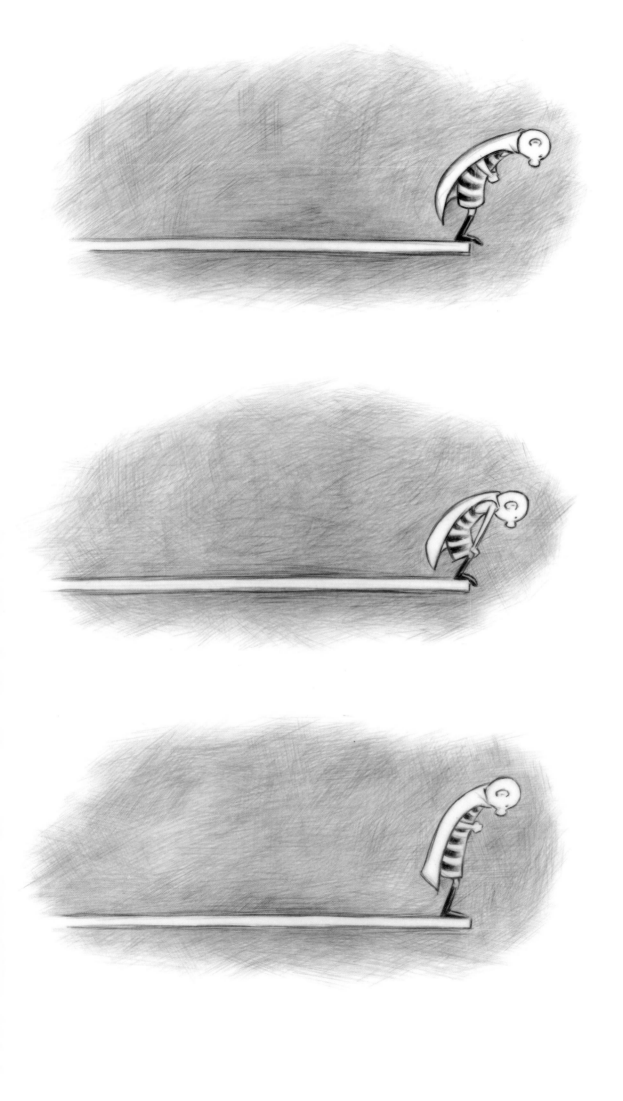

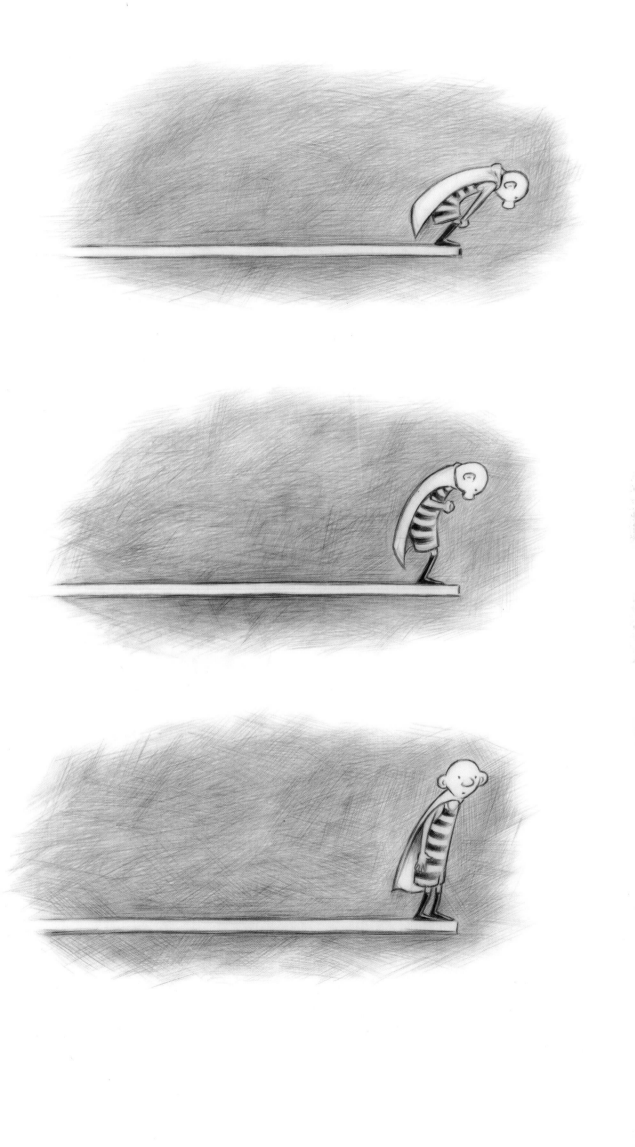

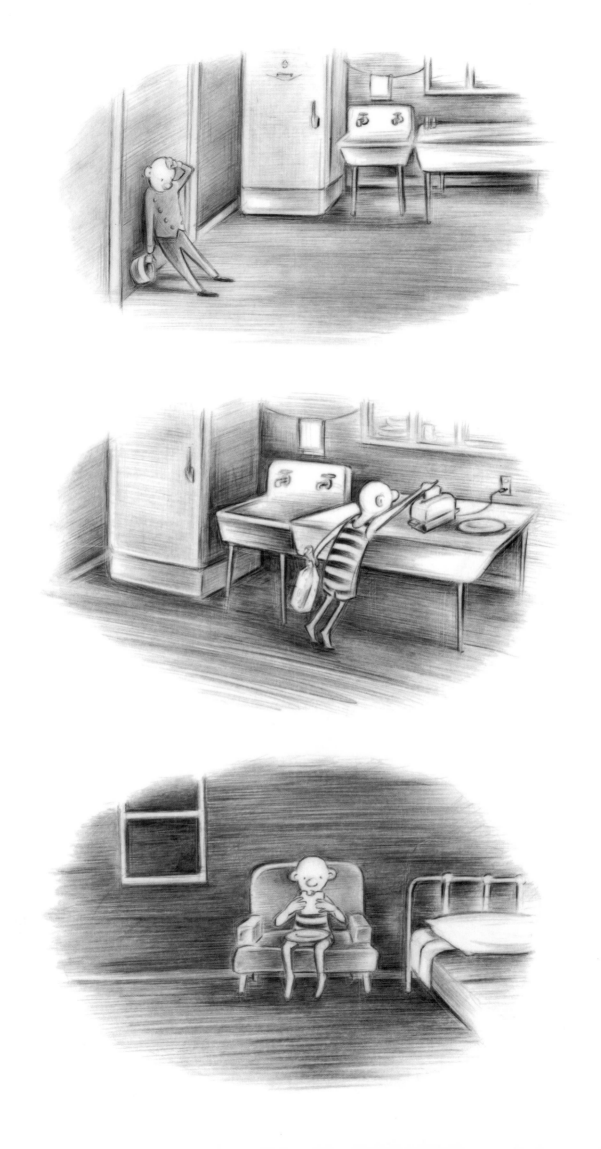

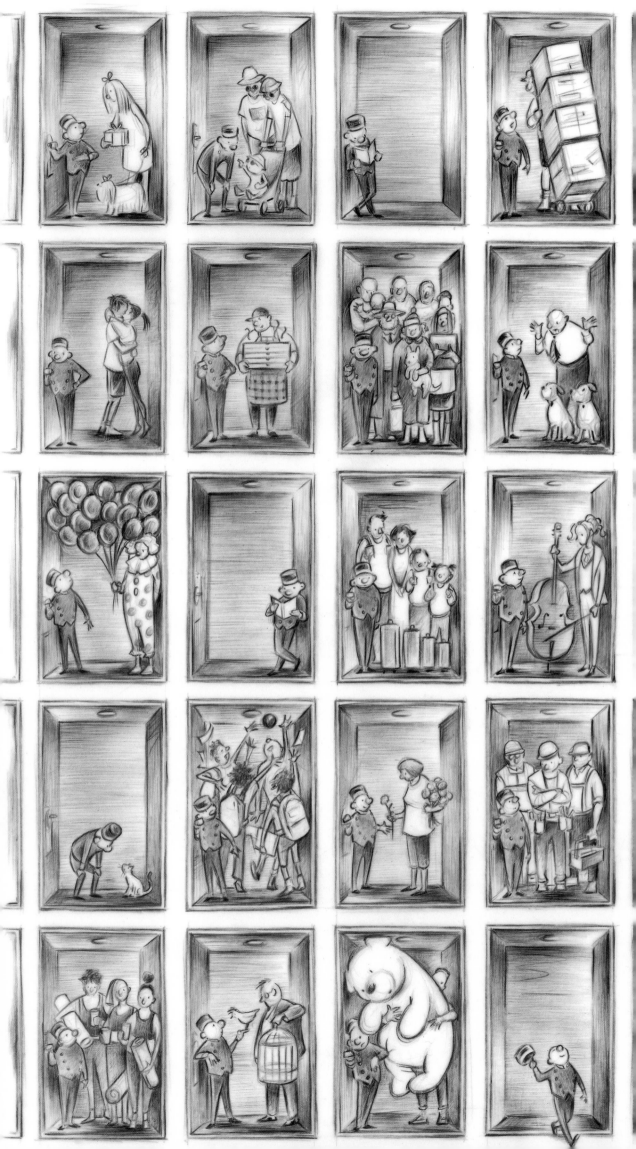

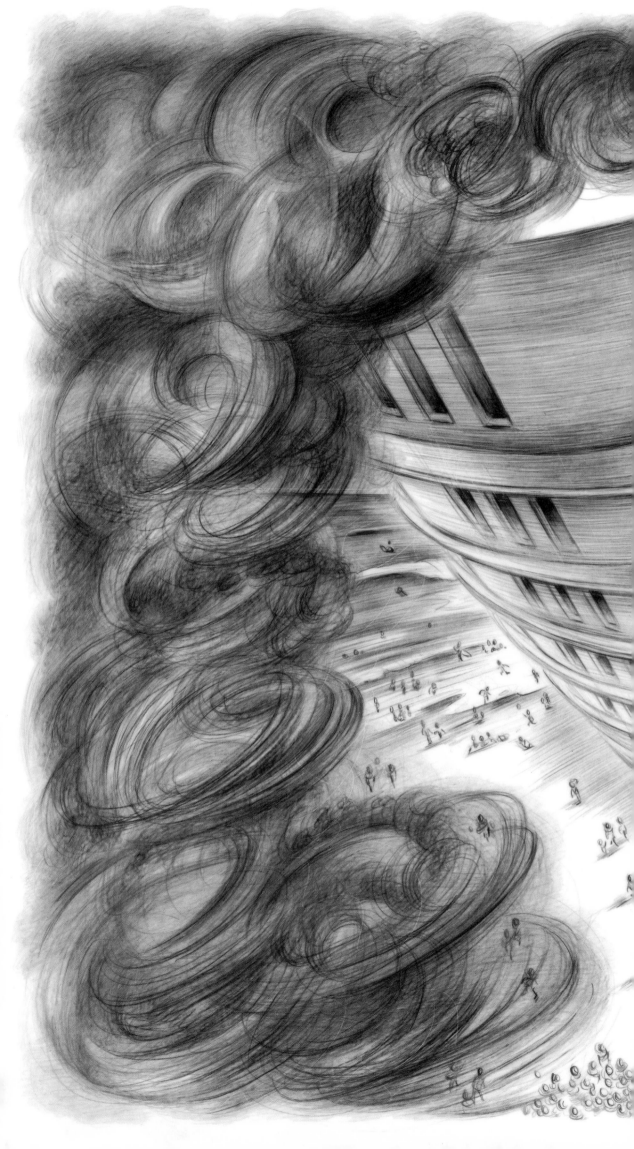

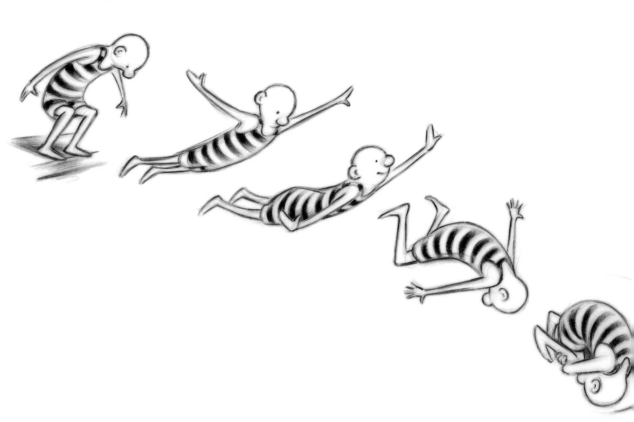

Behold!

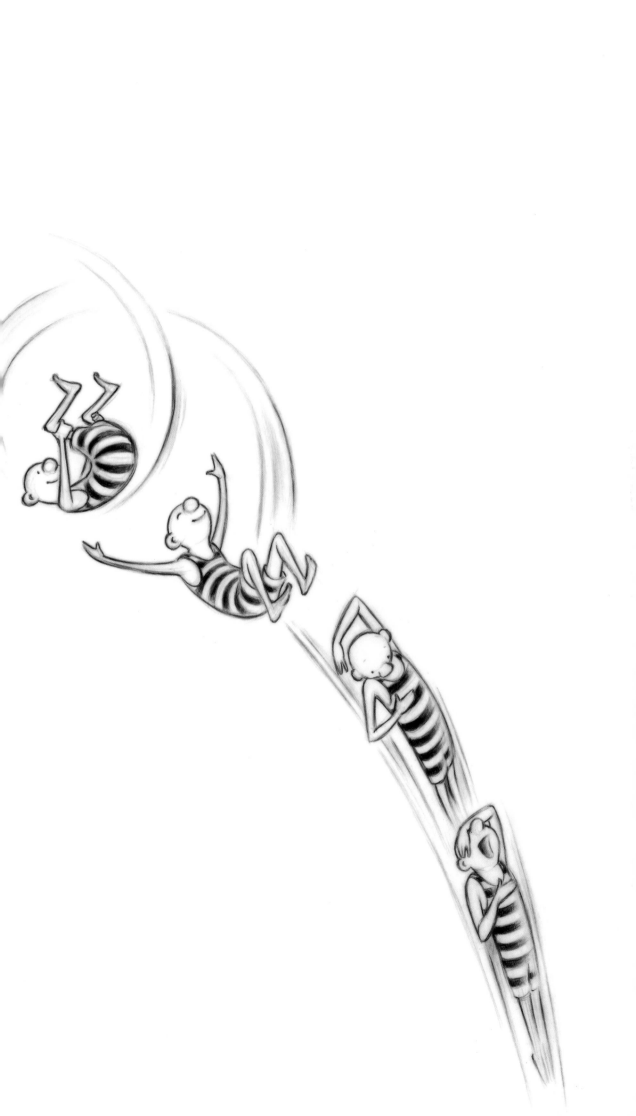

THE GREAT ZAPFINO!